Tabitha and Timothy Grow

Sarah Shackleton & Gillian Coulson

GW00374988

Tabitha and Timothy lived in a lovely house with a big yard.

They were very happy.

One day they decided to grow a flower in their yard.

So they planted some seeds and waited for the flower to grow.

And waited.

And waited.

But no flower grew.

So they planted more of their seeds.

And they waited.

And waited.

And waited.

But still no flower grew.

Tabitha and Timothy were very sad.

Then they heard about a kind lady
who might be able to help them.

They wrote a letter to the lady asking
if she had some seeds to help them
grow their flower.

And they waited.

And the kind lady wrote a letter back saying she would be delighted to help them.

The kind lady gave them some of her seeds to plant in their yard.

Tabitha and Timothy were very happy. They would be able to have their flower after all.

Tabitha and Timothy planted the seeds.

And they waited.

And waited.

And waited.

Then one day they saw a tiny shoot
growing out of the soil.

Tabitha and Timothy jumped up and
down with joy.

It was a miracle…
a flower was growing!

Tabitha and Timothy took great care of their little shoot.

They watered it and fed it and loved it.

And the shoot grew and grew until it became a big, beautiful flower.

Tabitha and Timothy were the happiest people in the world. They loved their flower more and more every single day.

And they were always grateful to the kind lady who helped make their dream come true.

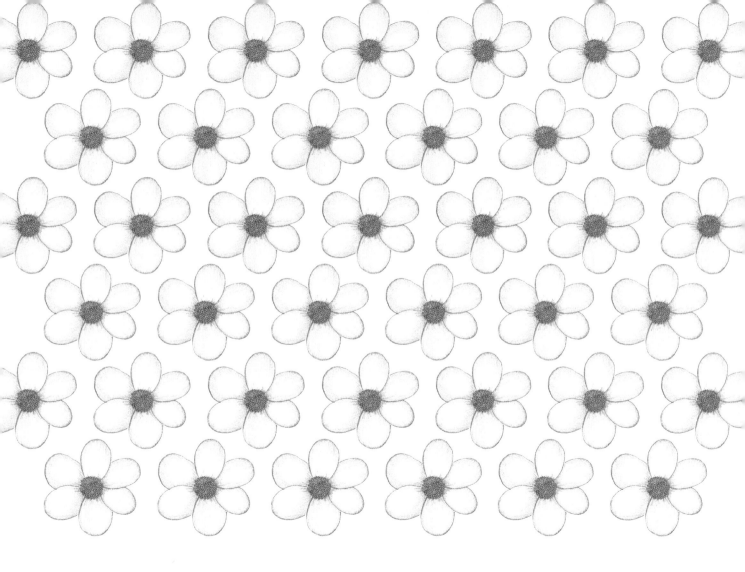

Printed in Great Britain
by Amazon